RORY the Dinosaur Wants a Pet

Liz Climo

Little, Brown and Company

New York   Boston

Rory is so excited!

He is going to play with his friends.

He says good-bye to Dad and is on his way.

Rory arrives at the beach and sees his friends Hank and Vera.

Hank has a surprise!

I got
a pet!
his
name
is Sheldon.

Sheldon is so much fun!

He likes to play fetch

and hide-and-seek.

They're having so much fun,
but it's time for his
friends to go home now.

Rory says good-bye.

On his walk home, Rory thinks about how fun Sheldon is.

I'm gonna find a pet too!

Rory begins to search for a pet.

He goes back to the beach, but all he finds are empty shells.

He looks in the jungle, but can't
reach any of the animals there.

Some animals are too fast.

Some are too busy.

And others don't want to be a pet at all.

It starts getting late, and Rory has
to go home for dinner.

DAD HE FOLLOWED ME HOME CAN I KEEP HIM?

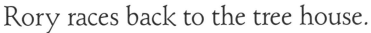

Rory races back to the tree house.

Rory names his new pet George.

George is so much fun!

Just like Sheldon, he likes to play fetch

good
job,
george!

and hide-and-seek.

He also loves playing dress up

and bath time.

It's time for bed now, so Rory
and George put their pajamas on.

Rory is so happy!

He wanted to find a pet to love

and one found him instead.

for

george

About This Book

The illustrations for this book were done with digital magic. The text was set in CG Schneidler, and the display type was hand-lettered by the author. This book was edited by Mary-Kate Gaudet and designed by Phil Caminiti with art direction by Dave Caplan and Saho Fujii. The production was supervised by Erika Schwartz, and the production editor was Annie McDonnell.

Thank you for your support of the author's rights. ❧ Little, Brown and Company ❧ Hachette Book Group ❧ 1290 Avenue of the Americas, New York, NY 10104 ❧ Visit us at lb-kids.com ❧ Little, Brown and Company is a division of Hachette Book Group, Inc. ❧ The Little, Brown name and logo are trademarks of Hachette Book Group, Inc. ❧ The publisher is not responsible for websites (or their content) that are not owned by the publisher. ❧ First Edition: June 2016 ❧ Library of Congress Cataloging-in-Publication Data ❧ Climo, Liz, author, illustrator. ❧ Rory the dinosaur gets a pet / by Liz Climo. — First edition. ❧ pages cm ❧ Summary: Rory the dinosaur wants a pet of his own and finds one in a coconut he names George. ❧ ISBN 978-0-316-27729-7 (hardcover) ❧ ISBN 978-0-316-39060-6 (international) ❧ [1. Dinosaurs—Fiction. 2. Pets—Fiction.] I. Title. ❧ PZ7.C622443Rm 2016 ❧ [E]—dc23 ❧ 2015008689 ❧ 10 9 8 7 6 5 4 3 2 1 ❧ APS ❧ PRINTED IN CHINA